The Mixed-up Message

adapted by Natalie Shaw
based on the screenplay "The Radio Message Mystery!"
written by Peter Sauder

Ready-to-Read

Simon Spotlight
New York   London   Toronto   Sydney

SIMON SPOTLIGHT
An imprint of Simon & Schuster Children's Publishing Division
1230 Avenue of the Americas, New York, New York 10020
Busytown Mysteries™ and all related and associated trademarks are owned by Cookie Jar Entertainment Inc. and
used under license from Cookie Jar Entertainment Inc. © 2011 Cookie Jar Entertainment Inc. All Rights Reserved.
All rights reserved, including the right of reproduction in whole or in part in any form.
SIMON SPOTLIGHT, READY-TO-READ, and colophon are registered trademarks of Simon & Schuster, Inc.
For information about special discounts for bulk purchases, please contact Simon & Schuster Special Sales at
1-866-506-1949 or business@simonandschuster.com.
Manufactured in the United States of America 0911 LAK
First Edition
2 4 6 8 10 9 7 5 3 1
ISBN 978-1-4424-2086-1

Huckle, Sally, and Lowly
are on a police boat.

They hear a horn blow.

Toot!

They wave hello to
a fishing boat!

The boat ride is over.
Sergeant Murphy gets a
radio message!

It sounds like a call for help.

"Goat . . . socks . . . help!"

What does that mean?

It is a mystery!

Goldbug reports the news about the call for help.

Who sent the message?

What does it mean?

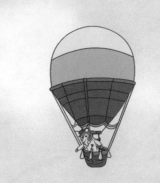

Pig Will thinks a goat needs help putting on socks.

Where can you find goats and socks?

There are goats at the farm.

There are socks at the

cleaners.

Sally asks the farmer if
he called for help with
his goats.

The farmer says he did
not call.
The goats are great!

The goats are late?

Late for what?

The goats are not late.

They are great.

Does the cleaner
need help
with socks?
No, he does not.

At the police station
they hear the
message again.
"Goat . . . socks . . . help!"

Now they hear birds and
waves, too!

Someone needs help at sea!

But why would goats
be at sea?
Maybe it only **sounds**
like goats.

What sounds like **goat**?

Note, coat, and . . . **boat**!

What sounds like **socks**?

Box, locks, and . . . **rocks**!

A boat was stuck on the rocks

Huckle solved the mystery!